PINGU

Published by BBC Books,
a division of BBC Enterprises Limited,
Woodlands, 80 Wood Lane, London W12 0TT
First published 1990
Illustrations by Tony Wolf
Original text by Sibylle von Flüe
Translated by Jenny Goodwin
English text edited by Helen Wire
This edition © BBC Books by arrangement with Dami Editore 1990
PINGU © Editoy A G Bertschikon ZH 1990
ISBN 0 563 36175 1
Set in 22/25 pt. Helvetica Regular by Goodfellow and Egan Ltd, Cambridge
Printed and bound in Great Britain by Cambus Litho Ltd, East Kilbride
Jacket printed by Belmont Press Ltd, Northampton

SRG SSR

PINGU

and the Seal

BBC BOOKS

PINGU GOES FISHING

This morning, Pingu said to his mum, "Today, I am
going to bring home some lovely fish for everyone."
He crosses the snow with his fishing rod and bucketful
of seaweed, until . . . he comes to a very steep slope!

But, Pingu doesn't give up easily. He finds a big piece
of ice and climbs on it. Giving himself a good push, he
begins to slide. Faster and faster, down he goes! Watch
out, Pingu! If you lose your balance, you'll end up on
your back with your legs in the air!

But Pingu makes it, safe and sound. At the bottom of the slope, he finds a hole in the ice. Like an expert fisherman, he puts a piece of seaweed on his hook and throws the line into the water. Then he sits down on a block of ice and waits.

"How easy it is for a good fisherman to catch fish!"
thinks Pingu as he places his first fish behind him.
"It's a shame that it's rather small. I hope the others
are bigger."
Pingu hasn't noticed there's a little seal watching him.

The next time Pingu throws the line, the little seal dives underwater. He removes the bait from the hook and replaces it with the first fish Pingu has caught. "Another one!" shouts Pingu excitedly. "This is really my lucky day."

The seal plays the same trick three times. Pingu is so thrilled to be catching so many fish, he doesn't even notice that it's always the same one. But, then the seal gives the line an extra hard pull!

"This fish must be enormous!" thinks Pingu. Suddenly, the line goes slack and Pingu almost falls down the hole! A chuckle from behind makes Pingu turn around. To his surprise, he sees the little seal happily eating up all his bait!

Not content with eating Pingu's bait, the playful seal throws a big snowball . . . SPLAT! This time Pingu is knocked head-first into the water!
Poor Pingu. He thought fishing was so easy!

The seal dives quickly out of sight underwater. But, it gives Pingu an idea. He hooks a piece of seaweed on to his line and hides.
"Now we'll see who is the cleverest!"
Slowly, he pulls the bait past the hole in the ice.

Just as the seal is about to take the bait, Pingu rushes from his hiding place and pounces on him.
Over and over, the two animals roll together in the snow. Are they cross with each other, or are they just playing?

In the struggle, the little seal hurts one of his flippers. Pingu tries to comfort him the best way he can. "Don't cry, little seal. We're friends now! And, you can have all the seaweed I have left if you like."

The seal stops crying and takes a mouthful of seaweed. Then, suddenly, he dives down the hole.
"Now, where's he gone?" wonders Pingu.
"To catch you a fish," says the seal, climbing out of the hole. And Pingu gives him all his seaweed.

"I have to go home now," says Pingu. "My mum is expecting me. Shall we play together, tomorrow?"
"Of course!" answers the seal with a wave.
What a lovely day! A beautiful big fish for his mum, and a new friend for Pingu.

PINGU AND THE PILE OF SNOW

The seal is making an old barrel into a sledge.
Pingu runs up to see what he is doing.
"What a fantastic idea! With all the snow that fell during
the night, we'll have a wonderful time."

Pingu sits inside the barrel and the seal pushes, stumbling along behind in the fresh snow. What hard work!

The seal soon says, "It's my turn, now." And then it is Pingu who pushes the sledge.

At last, there's a good downhill run!
Pingu gives a gentle push and jumps on to the sledge
behind the seal.
"Whoopee!" they both shriek with glee as the sledge
whooshes down the slope.

All too soon, the slope comes to an end. To do it again they must haul the sledge back up to the top. Pingu pulls from above, while the seal pushes from behind. "Keep going," pants Pingu. "We're almost there."

The second time they come down, the sledge goes even faster. It's tremendous fun!
But, then, the sledge slithers out of control! They only just miss crashing into a very large pile of snow!

This time, the seal climbs along to the top of the hill. He passes a rope around a big block of ice and throws one end down to Pingu.

"Tie it on to the sledge," he shouts to his friend waiting below.

Holding on to the other end of the rope, the seal starts down the slope. And, up comes Pingu on the sledge! The two friends wave as they pass each other halfway. They are very pleased with themselves for having such a brilliant idea.

Just then, the seal loses his grip on the rope!
Suddenly, Pingu and the sledge are plummeting
backwards towards a large pile of snow!
"Pingu, Pingu!" cries the horrified seal. "Where are
you? Oohhh!"

There's not the slightest trace of Pingu, or the sledge!
The seal hardly knows where to look, until, "Help, I'm
here!" he hears a faint cry from beneath a huge pile of
snow. He begins digging frantically and finds . . . one of
Pingu's flippers!

The seal rushes to get help.
"Hurry, please!" he begs. "There's an emergency.
Pingu has had a terrible accident."
"I'll be right with you," answers the doctor, running
inside to collect his first-aid kit.

They are soon speeding to the rescue.
With special snow shoes for himself and the stretcher,
the doctor travels very fast. And, so does the seal who
is guiding the way!

There are still faint cries coming from the pile of snow.
The doctor quickly heaves up a heavy block of ice so
that the seal can, at last, pull his friend free!
Fortunately, Pingu is not seriously hurt, though he does
look rather weak.

The doctor lets the seal ride with Pingu on the stretcher.
"Come on, I'm taking you two home. You've had quite
enough excitement for one day."
"It has been fun, hasn't it?" whispers the seal to Pingu,
happy that his friend is not hurt.

A STRANGE GAME

"What a lovely sleep," says Pingu, yawning.

"Hey!" someone calls.

"Who's that?" asks the penguin, sitting up.

"It's me!" His friend is there behind the snowman.

"I've come to show you a new game," says the seal, bringing out a lovely fish.
He throws the fish up into the air and catches it on his nose, balancing it very skilfully.
"Well done!" says Pingu, clapping his flippers

"It's not easy, you know," says the seal, "but, I'm very good at it."
"Well, then, let's see if you can catch this!" shouts Pingu, throwing the fish into the air. But, the seal catches the fish on the end of his nose and returns it.

The fish knocks Pingu to the ground. The seal rolls over
on to the ice, laughing so much he has to hold his
stomach.
"You were right. You are really good at it," says Pingu
enviously. "Can you show me how to do it?"

"Of course I'll show you," says the seal and patiently begins teaching Pingu what to do.
Pingu listens carefully, tries, and drops it. He tries again and again until he masters it. It's not long before he's almost as good as the seal!

Whoops! Now, Pingu has a problem. The fish is not balanced skilfully on his nose, it's stuck on his head! Poor Pingu. He still has a lot to learn.
"Help," he cries, trying to shake the fish off.

All that head shaking only fixes the fish more firmly.
Pingu's head is nearly swallowed by the fish's mouth.
"Heave . . . ho!" shouts his friend and, using all his
strength, the seal manages to free Pingu of his
uncomfortable hat.

"Let's play volley ball, instead," suggests the seal.
Pingu thinks that sounds like a much better idea.
The fish is soon flying backwards and forwards
between them. Both players are so good, they don't
drop the fish in the snow even once!

Suddenly, the fish gets caught on the rope! They try everything they can think of to knock it down. They try jumping but it's too high. They throw snowballs but they miss. They wobble the poles. But, still, the fish remains very firmly struck.

Pingu even shins up the pole. Just as he is about to reach for the fish, he slips and ends up in the snow with his legs in the air!
"You poor thing," says the seal but he can't stop himself from laughing.

"Hey, I've got an idea!" says Pingu and runs off towards his igloo. There, leaning against the wall, are two strange-looking sticks. Pingu will soon have that fish off the rope!

On his stilts, Pingu is even taller than his daddy.
And, now, he can easily reach the fish! With one
carefully aimed flick of his flipper, he tips the fish off the
rope. PLOP!

"Do you know, Pingu," says the seal, "after all this exercise, I'm feeling rather hungry."
"So am I," replies Pingu. "Let's have some tea."
Poor fish – first he's their ball; now he's their tea!